Help, Help, Little Frog!

A Little Animal Adventure

Help, Help
Little Frog!

Written by Christina Wilsdon
Illustrations by John Carrozza

Published by The Reader's Digest Association Limited
London ❖ New York ❖ Sydney ❖ Montreal

'Wheeee!' cried Little Frog as she hopped from lily pad to lily pad.

'What a happy little hopper you are today!' said her mother.

Little Frog's answer was an extra-long jump to another lily pad.

Little Frog was about to leap into the air again when she heard a tiny voice cry, 'Help!'

'Who's there?' Little Frog called out. She looked around slowly and saw a caterpillar perched on a rock. He waved a few of his legs at her.

'The wind blew me out of my tree and onto
this rock. I can't swim! Can you help me to get
back to shore?' asked the caterpillar.

Little Frog hesitated. 'I want to hop and have fun,' she thought. 'I don't want to be a ferry boat and carry passengers.'

But then she saw the sad, worried look in the caterpillar's eyes. She thought about how she would feel if she were far from home with no way to get back. So Little Frog replied, 'Hop aboard!'

She giggled as the caterpillar crawled onto her back. 'That tickles.'

Little Frog jumped from lily pad to lily pad with short, gentle hops. 'Everything OK back there?' she asked the caterpillar.

'Yes!' replied the caterpillar.

The caterpillar groaned. 'I really want to get back to my tree quickly,' he said to Little Frog.

'You were glad to get help,' Little Frog pointed out. 'Now Ladybird needs help, too.'

She stretched out her leg to help the ladybird climb aboard.

Little Frog continued hopping across the pond. She heard a third tiny voice cry, 'Help!'

'Not again!' complained the caterpillar.

Little Frog spied a snail clinging to the stem of a plant.

'Can you help me?' asked the snail. 'I'm so slow, it will take me days to reach the shore!'

The ladybird and caterpillar grumbled, but Little Frog said, 'Hop aboard!'

Hop. Hop. Hop. Little Frog leapt from lily pad to lily pad.

'Phew!' said Little Frog to herself. 'I'm getting tired of hopping with all this extra weight on my back. And the shore still looks so far away!'

'Are we there yet?' asked the caterpillar.

'No,' replied Little Frog as she flopped onto a rock to rest.

'Do you think Little Frog is getting tired?' asked the snail.

'I think so,' said the ladybird. 'Perhaps we should get off and let her rest.'

They all crawled off Little Frog onto the rock.

Suddenly, the rock began to rise.

'Oops!' cried Little Frog. 'It looks like I've landed on a turtle's shell instead of a rock!'

The turtle smiled at Little Frog.

'That's all right. You were very kind to help these animals. Now you rest and I'll carry everyone to the shore,' he said.

Little Frog rested while the turtle swam to shore. The caterpillar, ladybird and snail crawled off the turtle's shell. They thanked the turtle and Little Frog.

'Yes, thank you!' said Little Frog to the turtle, as she hopped off the turtle's back. 'You are very kind, too.'

The turtle waved goodbye as Little Frog sprang into the air and landed in the water, making a great big splash for such a little frog.

All about ... FROGS

IN OR OUT?
Frogs can live both in the water and on land, but usually stay in or close to water.

IN THE BEGINNING...
Most frogs start life as a tadpole in water. A tadpole has a long tail and no legs. Over time, it loses its tail and grows legs, gradually changing into a frog.

FACT FILE

STICKY MITTS
Tree frogs have sticky pads on their long toes. The pads help them cling to branches.

Did know?

A PUFF ...

Although small in size, frogs can be very loud! Many kinds of frogs puff up with air, which makes their croaking sounds much louder. The spring peeper, shown here, has a throat that blows up like a balloon when it sings!

... AND A HOP!

Frogs are great jumpers and swimmers. Their back legs are especially strong for jumping, and their webbed feet help them to swim.

Reader's Digest
YOUNG FAMILIES

Help, Help Little Frog! is a Little Animal Adventures book
published by Reader's Digest Young Families, Inc.
by arrangement with Éditions Nathan, Paris, France

Written by Christina Wilsdon
Illustrations by John Carrozza
Notebook artwork © Paul Bommer

Senior Designer: Wendy Boccuzzi
Editor: Sharon Yates
Editorial Director: Pamela Pia

This edition was adapted and published in 2008 by
The Reader's Digest Association Limited
11 Westferry Circus, Canary Wharf, London E14 4HE

We are committed to both the quality of our products
and the service we provide to our customers.
We value your comments, so please feel free to contact us on
08705 113366 or via our website at:
www.readersdigest.co.uk
If you have any comments or suggestions about the content of our books,
you can contact us at: gbeditorial@readersdigest.co.uk

Printed in China

Book code: 637-014 UP0000-2
ISBN: 978 0 276 44241 4